# Q is for

## AN ALPHABET

**by Mary Elting
& Michael Folsom
Pictures by Jack Kent**

# Duck

## GUESSING GAME

Clarion Books / New York

*P is for Jamie and S is for Raphael*

Clarion Books
a Houghton Mifflin Company imprint
215 Park Avenue South, New York, NY 10003
Text copyright © 1980 by Mary Elting and Michael Folsom
Illustrations copyright © 1980 by Jack Kent
Reprinted with full-color illustrations, 2005.

The illustrations were executed in pen and ink and digital media.
Illustrations colorized by Michelle Gengaro-Kokmen.
The text was set in 29-point Miller Text Roman.

www.houghtonmifflinbooks.com

Printed in Singapore

The Library of Congress catalogued the original hardcover edition as follows:

Elting, Mary, 1906–
Q is for duck.
Summary: While learning some facts about animals, the reader is challenged to guess why A is for zoo, B is for dog, and C is for hen.
[1. Alphabet. 2. Animals] I. Folsom, Michael, joint author.
II. Kent, Jack, 1920– III. Title.
PZ7.E53Qab      [E]       80-13854
ISBN   0-395-29437-1

CL ISBN-13: 978-0-618-57389-9   CL ISBN-10: 0-618-57389-5
PA ISBN-13: 978-0-618-57412-4   PA ISBN-10: 0-618-57412-3

TWP 10 9 8 7 6 5

# A is for Zoo

TICKETS

ZOO ENTRANCE →

Why?

Because . . .

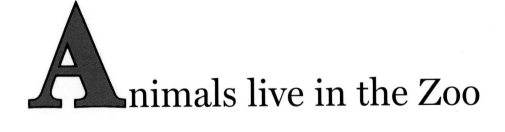

Animals live in the Zoo

# B is for Dog

Why?

Because a Dog **B**arks

# C is for Hen

Why?

Because a Hen **C**lucks

 **D** is for Mole

Why?

Because a Mole **D**igs

E is for Whale

Why?

Because . . .

a Whale is Enormous

F is for Bird

Why?

Because a Bird **F**lies

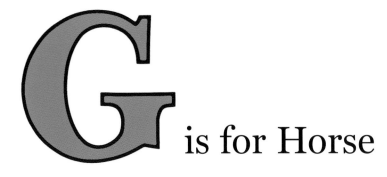 **G** is for Horse

Why?

Because a Horse Gallops

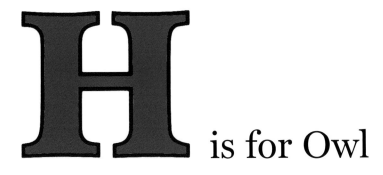 is for Owl

Why?

Because an Owl **H**oots

Because
Mosquito bites Itch

# J

is for Kangaroo

Why?

Because a Kangaroo Jumps

# K is for Mule

Why?

Because a Mule **K**icks

**L** is for Frog

Why?

Because a Frog Leaps

# M is for Cow

Why?

Because a Cow **M**oos

# N is for Cat

Why?

Because a cat **N**aps

O is for Pig

Why?

Because a Pig **O**inks

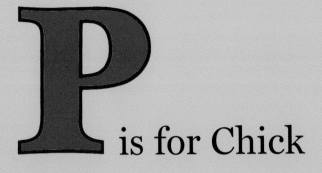

P is for Chick

Why?

Because a Chick **P**eeps

# Q is for Duck

Why?

Because a Duck **Q**uacks

# R is for Lion

Why?

Because a Lion **R**oars

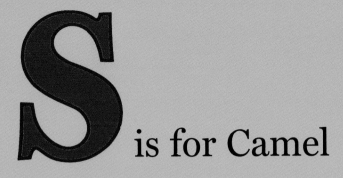

**S** is for Camel

Why?

Because a Camel Spits

# T is for Elephant

Why?

Because an Elephant **T**rumpets

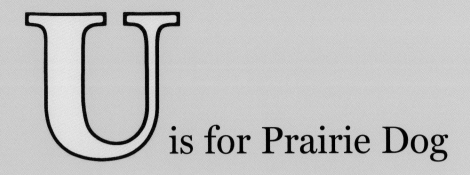

U is for Prairie Dog

Why?

Because Prairie Dogs live

Underground

V is for Chameleon

Why?

Because a
Chameleon seems to Vanish

**W**is for Snake

Why?

Because a Snake iggles

**X** is for Dinosaur

Why?

Because Dinosaurs are

e**X**tinct

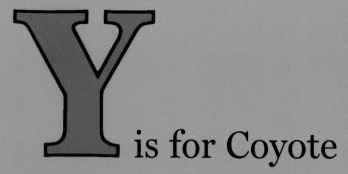

Y is for Coyote

Because a Coyote Yowls

# Z is for Animals

Why?

Because
Animals live in the $\mathbf{Z}$oo